7

Pink Bunny

Level 2F

Written by Lucy George
Illustrated by Valentina Mendicino

What is synthetic phonics?

Synthetic phonics teaches children to recognise the sounds of letters and to blend (synthesise) them together to make whole words.

Understanding sound/letter relationships gives children the confidence and ability to read unfamiliar words, without having to rely on memory or guesswork; this helps them progress towards independent reading.

Did you know? Spoken English uses more than 40 speech sounds. Each sound is called a *phoneme*. Some phonemes relate to a single letter (d-o-g) and others to combinations of letters (sh-ar-p). When a phoneme is written down it is called a *grapheme*. Teaching these sounds, matching them to their written form and sounding out words for reading is the basis of synthetic phonics.

Consultant

I love reading phonics has been created in consultation with language expert Abigail Steel. She has a background in teaching and teacher training and is a respected expert in the field of Synthetic Phonics. Abigail Steel is a regular contributor to educational publications. Her international education consultancy supports parents and teachers in the promotion of literacy skills.

Reading tips

This book focuses on the sound:
nk as in 'sunk'

Tricky words in this book

Any words in bold do not sound exactly as they look (don't fit the usual sound-letter rules) or are new and have not yet been introduced.

Tricky words in this book:

her to the now
have done like goes

Extra ways to have fun with this book

After the reader has read the story, ask them questions about what they have just read:

What were Daddy and Harry doing in the garden?
Where did Harry wash Bunny?

Explain that the two letters 'nk' make one sound. Think of other words that use the 'nk' sound, such as stink and brink.

I can be
a bit clumsy sometimes.
I have to look out to
avoid accidents!

A pronunciation guide

This grid contains the sounds used in
the story and a guide on how to say them.

s as in sat	a as in ant	t as in tin	p as in pig	i as in ink
n as in net	c as in cat	e as in egg	h as in hen	r as in rat
m as in mug	d as in dog	g as in get	o as in ox	u as in up
l as in log	f as in fan	b as in bag	j as in jug	v as in van
w as in wet	z as in zip	y as in yet	k as in kit	qu as in quick
x as in box	ff as in off	ll as in ball	ss as in kiss	zz as in buzz
ck as in duck	pp as in puppy	nn as in bunny	rr as in arrow	gg as in egg
dd as in daddy	bb as in chubby	tt as in attic	sh as in shop	ch as in chip
th as in them	th as in thin	ng as in sing	nk as in sunk	

Be careful not to add an 'uh' sound to 's', 't', 'p',
'c', 'h', 'r', 'm', 'd', 'g', 'l', 'f' and 'b'. For example,
say 'fff' not 'fuh' and 'sss' not 'suh'.

Bunny is in **her** box. Harry and
Daddy kick a ball.

Daddy misses **the** net!

The ball zips in **to** the box.

'Clink, clank, clunk!' The box falls.

Pink paint **goes** all over Bunny.

Bunny looks **like** a punk!

Daddy and Harry must wash the
pink off quick!

Harry and Daddy fill the sink.

Harry dunks Bunny in the sink.

Bunny gets all wet.

Bunny is slippery, but Harry can't
let Bunny sink.

Harry rubs Bunny dry.

Bunny is dazzling!

Harry and Daddy put Bunny back
in her box.

Bunny is all fluffy and chubby!
Harry thinks Bunny looked
better pink!

The job is **done**. Daddy and Harry **have** a drink.

'Clink, clank, clunk!'

The dog runs around. He's all pink,

and he stinks!

So **now** Harry and Daddy wash the dog in the sink!

OVER **48** TITLES IN SIX LEVELS
Abigail Steel recommends...

Other titles to enjoy from Level 2

I love reading phonics **Chuck and Duck**	I love reading phonics **Let's go to the Swings**	I love reading phonics **Wish Fish**
978-1-84898-387-8	978-1-84898-549-0	978-1-84898-386-1

Some titles from Level 1

I love reading phonics **Bad Rat**	I love reading phonics **The Best Gift**	I love reading phonics **Clint and Grant Play I-Spy**	I love reading phonics **Gran and Bret's Trip**
978-1-84898-277-2	978-1-84898-396-0	978-1-84898-548-3	978-1-84898-547-6

Some titles from Level 3

I love reading phonics **Bart's Go-Cart**	I love reading phonics **Queen Ella's Feet**	I love reading phonics **Puff Flies**	I love reading phonics **The Pop Duet**
978-1-84898-552-0	978-1-84898-398-4	978-1-84898-399-1	978-1-84898-551-3

An Hachette UK Company
www.hachette.co.uk

Copyright © Octopus Publishing Group Ltd 2012
First published in Great Britain in 2012 by TickTock, a division of Octopus Publishing Group Ltd,
Endeavour House, 189 Shaftesbury Avenue, London WC2H 8JY.
www.octopusbooks.co.uk

ISBN 978 1 84898 550 6

Printed and bound in China
10 9 8 7 6 5 4 3 2 1

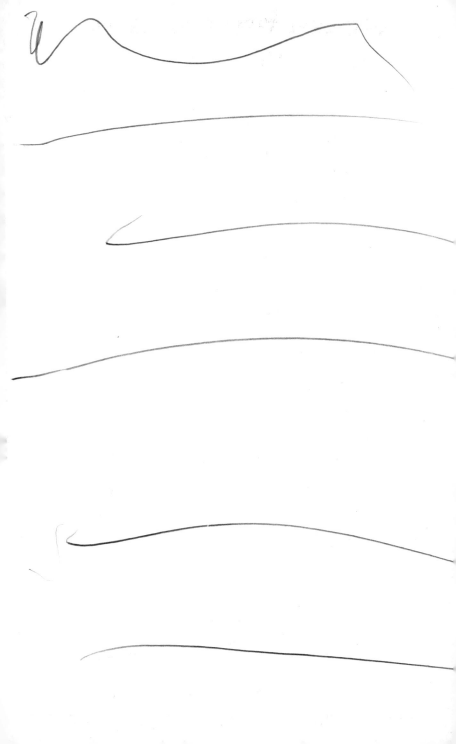